CU00497409

Honore de Balzac

Paz

Honore de Balzac

Paz

1st Edition | ISBN: 978-3-73408-329-7

Place of Publication: Frankfurt am Main, Germany

Year of Publication: 2019

Outlook Verlag GmbH, Germany.

PAZ

(La Fausse Maitresse)
By Honore De Balzac

Translated by Katharine Prescott Wormeley

DEDICATION

Dedicated to the Comtesse Clara Maffei.

Contents

PAZ

(LA FAUSSE MAITRESSE)

I

In September, 1835, one of the richest heiresses of the faubourg Saint-Germain, Mademoiselle du Rouvre, the only daughter of the Marquis du Rouvre, married Comte Adam Mitgislas Laginski, a young Polish exile.

We ask permission to write these Polish names as they are pronounced, to spare our readers the aspect of the fortifications of consonants by which the Slave language protects its vowels,—probably not to lose them, considering how few there are.

The Marquis du Rouvre had squandered nearly the whole of a princely fortune, which he obtained originally through his marriage with a Demoiselle de Ronquerolles. Therefore, on her mother's side Clementine du Rouvre had the Marquis de Ronquerolles for uncle, and Madame de Serizy for aunt. On her father's side she had another uncle in the eccentric person of the Chevalier du Rouvre, a younger son of the house, an old bachelor who had become very rich by speculating in lands and houses. The Marquis de Ronquerolles had the misfortune to lose both his children at the time of the cholera, and the only son of Madame de Serizy, a young soldier of great promise, perished in Africa in the affair of the Makta. In these days rich families stand between the danger of impoverishing their children if they have too many, or of extinguishing their names if they have too few,—a singular result of the Code which Napoleon never thought of. By a curious turn of fortune Clementine became, in spite of her father having squandered his substance on Florine (one of the most charming actresses in Paris), a great heiress. The Marquis de Ronquerolles, a clever diplomatist under the new dynasty, his sister, Madame de Serizy, and the Chevalier du Rouvre agreed, in order to save their fortunes from the dissipations of the marquis, to settle them on their niece, to whom, moreover, they each pledged themselves to pay ten thousand francs a year from the day of her marriage.

It is quite unnecessary to say that the Polish count, though an exile, was no expense to the French government. Comte Adam Laginski belonged to one of the oldest and most illustrious families in Poland, which was allied to many of the princely houses of Germany,—Sapieha, Radziwill, Mniszech, Rzewuski, Czartoryski, Leczinski, Lubormirski, and all the other great Sarmatian SKIS. But heraldic knowledge is not the most distinguishing feature of the French nation under Louis-Philippe, and Polish nobility was no great recommendation to the bourgeoisie who were lording it in those days. Besides, when Adam first made his appearance, in 1833, on the boulevard des Italiens, at Frascati, and at the Jockey-Club, he was leading the life of a young man who, having lost his political prospects, was taking his pleasure in Parisian dissipation. At first he was thought to be a student.

The Polish nationality had at this period fallen as low in French estimation, thanks to a shameful governmental reaction, as the republicans had sought to raise it. The singular struggle of the Movement against Resistance (two words which will be inexplicable thirty years hence) made sport of what ought to have been truly respected,—the name of a conquered nation to whom the French had offered hospitality, for whom fetes had been given (with songs and dances by subscription), above all, a nation which in the Napoleonic struggle between France and Europe had given us six thousand men, and what men!

Do not infer from this that either side is taken here; either that of the Emperor Nicholas against Poland, or that of Poland against the Emperor. It would be a foolish thing to slip political discussion into tales that are intended to amuse or interest. Besides, Russia and Poland were both right,—one to wish the unity of its empire, the other to desire its liberty. Let us say in passing that Poland might have conquered Russia by the influence of her morals instead of fighting her with weapons; she should have imitated China which, in the end, Chinesed the Tartars, and will, it is to be hoped, Chinese the English. Poland ought to have Polonized Russia. Poniatowski tried to do so in the least favorable portion of the empire; but as a king he was little understood,—because, possibly, he did not fully understand himself.

But how could the Parisians avoid disliking an unfortunate people who were the cause of that shameful falsehood enacted during the famous review at which all Paris declared its will to succor Poland? The Poles were held up to them as the allies of the republican party, and they never once remembered that Poland was a republic of aristocrats. From that day forth the bourgeoisie treated with base contempt the exiles of the nation it had worshipped a few days earlier. The wind of a riot is always enough to veer the Parisians from north to south under any regime. It is necessary to remember these sudden fluctuations of feeling in order to understand why it was that in 1835 the word "Pole" conveyed a derisive meaning to a people who consider themselves the wittiest and most courteous nation on earth, and their city of Paris the focus of enlightenment, with the sceptre of arts and literature within its grasp.

There are, alas! two sorts of Polish exiles,—the republican Poles, sons of Lelewel, and the noble Poles, at the head of whom is Prince Adam Czartoryski. The two classes are like fire and water; but why complain of that? Such divisions are always to be found among exiles, no matter of what nation they may be, or in what countries they take refuge. They carry their countries and their hatreds with them. Two French priests, who had emigrated to Brussels during the Revolution, showed the utmost horror of each other, and when one of them was asked why, he replied with a glance at his companion in misery: "Why? because he's a Jansenist!" Dante would gladly have stabbed a Guelf had he met him in exile. This explains the virulent attacks of the French against the venerable Prince Adam Czartoryski, and the dislike shown to the better class of Polish exiles by the shopkeeping Caesars and the licensed Alexanders of Paris.

In 1834, therefore, Adam Mitgislas Laginski was something of a butt for Parisian pleasantry.

"He is rather nice, though he is a Pole," said Rastignac.

"All these Poles pretend to be great lords," said Maxime de Trailles, "but this one does pay his gambling debts, and I begin to think he must have property."

Without wishing to offend these banished men, it may be allowable to remark that the light-hearted, careless inconsistency of the Sarmatian character does justify in some degree the satire of the Parisians, who, by the bye, would behave in like circumstances exactly as the Poles do. The French aristocracy, so nobly succored during the Revolution by the Polish lords, certainly did not return the kindness in 1832. Let us have the melancholy courage to admit this, and to say that the faubourg Saint-Germain is still the debtor of Poland.

Was Comte Adam rich, or was he poor, or was he an adventurer? This problem was long unsolved. The diplomatic salons, faithful to instructions, imitated the silence of the Emperor Nicholas, who held that all Polish exiles were virtually dead and buried. The court of the Tuileries, and all who took their cue from it, gave striking proof of the political quality which was then dignified by the name of sagacity. They turned their backs on a Russian prince with whom they had all been on intimate terms during the Emigration, merely because it was said that the Emperor Nicholas gave him the cold shoulder. Between the caution of the court and the prudence of the diplomates, the Polish exiles of distinction lived in Paris in the Biblical solitude of "super flumina Babylonis," or else they haunted a few salons which were the neutral ground of all opinions. In a city of pleasure, like Paris, where amusements abound on all sides, the heedless gayety of a Pole finds twice as many encouragements as it needs to a life of dissipation.

It must be said, however, that Adam had two points against him,—his appearance, and his mental equipment. There are two species of Pole, as there are two species of Englishwoman. When an Englishwoman is not very handsome she is horribly ugly. Comte Adam belonged in the second category of human beings. His small face, rather sharp in expression, looked as if it had been pressed in a vise. His short nose, and fair hair, and reddish beard and moustache made him look all the more like a goat because he was small and thin, and his tarnished yellow eyes caught you with that oblique look which Virgil celebrates. How came he, in spite of such obvious disadvantages, to possess really exquisite manners and a distinguished air? The problem is solved partly by the care and elegance of his dress, and partly by the training given him by his mother, a Radziwill. His courage amounted to daring, but his mind was not more than was needed for the ephemeral talk and pleasantry of Parisian conversation. And yet it would have been difficult to find among the young men of fashion in Paris a single one who was his superior. Young men talk a great deal too much in these days of horses, money, taxes, deputies; French *conversation* is no longer what it was. Brilliancy of mind needs leisure and certain social inequalities to bring it out. There is, probably, more real conversation in Vienna or St. Petersburg than in Paris. Equals do not need to employ delicacy or shrewdness in speech; they blurt out things as they are. Consequently the dandies of Paris did not discover the great seigneur in the rather heedless young fellow who, in their talks, would flit from one subject to another, all the more intent upon amusement because he had just escaped from a great peril, and, finding himself in a city where his family was unknown, felt at liberty to lead a loose life without the risk of disgracing his name.

But one fine day in 1834 Adam suddenly bought a house in the rue de la Pepiniere. Six months later his style of living was second to none in Paris. About the time when he thus began to take himself seriously he had seen Clementine du Rouvre at the Opera and had fallen in love with her. A year later the marriage took place. The salon of Madame d'Espard was the first to sound his praises. Mothers of daughters then learned too late that as far back as the year 900 the family of the Laginski was among the most illustrious of the North. By an act of prudence which was very unPolish, the mother of the young count had mortgaged her entire property on the breaking out of the insurrection for an immense sum lent by two Jewish bankers in Paris. Comte Adam was now in possession of eighty thousand francs a year. When this was discovered society ceased to be surprised at the imprudence which had been laid to the charge of Madame de Serizy, the Marquis de Ronquerolles, and the Chevalier du Rouvre in yielding to the foolish passion of their niece. People jumped, as usual, from one extreme of judgment to the other.

During the winter of 1836 Comte Adam was the fashion, and Clementine Laginska one of the queens of Paris. Madame Laginska is now a member of that charming circle of young women represented by Mesdames de Lestorade, de Portenduere, Marie de Vandenesse, du Guenic, and de Maufrigneuse, the flowers of our present Paris, who live at such immeasurable distance from the parvenus, the vulgarians, and the speculators of the new regime.

This preamble is necessary to show the sphere in which was done one of those noble actions, less rare than the calumniators of our time admit,—actions which, like pearls, the fruit of pain and suffering, are hidden within rough shells, lost in the gulf, the sea, the tossing waves of what we call society, the century, Paris, London, St. Petersburg,—or what you will.

If the axiom that architecture is the expression of manner and morals was ever proved, it was certainly after the insurrection of 1830, during the present reign of the house of Orleans. As all the old fortunes are diminishing in France, the majestic mansions of our ancestors are constantly being demolished and replaced by species of phalansteries, in which the peers of July occupy the third floor above some newly enriched empirics on the lower floors. A mixture of styles is confusedly employed. As there is no longer a real court or nobility to give the tone, there is no harmony in the production of art. Never, on the other hand, has architecture discovered so many economical ways of imitating the real and the solid, or displayed more resources, more talent, in distributing them. Propose to an architect to build upon the garden at the back of an old mansion, and he will run you up a little Louvre overloaded with ornament. He will manage to get in a courtyard, stables, and if you care for it, a garden. Inside the house he will accommodate a quantity of little rooms and passages. He is so clever in deceiving the eye that you think you will have plenty of space; but it is only a nest of small rooms, after all, in which a ducal family has to turn itself about in the space that its own bakehouse formerly occupied.

The hotel of the Comtesse Laginska, rue de la Pepiniere, is one of these creations, and stands between court and garden. On the right, in the court, are the kitchens and offices; to the left the coachhouse and stables. The porter's lodge is between two charming portes-cocheres. The chief luxury of the house is a delightful greenhouse contrived at the end of a boudoir on the ground-floor which opens upon an admirable suite of reception rooms. An English philanthropist had built this architectural bijou, designed the garden, added the greenhouse, polished the doors, bricked the courtyard, painted the window-frames green, and realized, in short, a dream which resembled (proportions excepted) George the Fourth's Pavilion at Brighton. The inventive and industrious Parisian workmen had moulded the doors and window-frames; the ceilings were imitated from the middle-ages or those of a Venetian palace; marble veneering abounded on the outer walls. Steinbock and Francois Souchet had designed the mantel-pieces and the panels above the doors; Schinner had painted the ceilings in his masterly manner. The beauties of the staircase, white as a woman's arm, defied those of the hotel Rothschild. On account of the riots and the unsettled times, the cost of this folly was only about eleven hundred thousand francs,—to an Englishman a mere nothing. All this luxury, called princely by persons who do not know what real princes are, was built in the garden of the house of a purveyor made a Croesus by the Revolution, who had escaped to Brussels and died there after going into bankruptcy. The Englishman died in Paris, of Paris; for to many persons Paris is a disease,—sometimes several diseases. His widow, a Methodist, had a horror of the little nabob establishment, and ordered it to be sold. Comte Adam bought it at a bargain; and how he came to do so shall presently be made known, for bargains were not at all in his line as a grand seigneur.

Behind the house lay the verdant velvet of an English lawn shaded at the lower end by a clump of exotic trees, in the midst of which stood a Chinese pagoda with soundless belfries and motionless golden eggs. The greenhouse concealed the garden wall on the northern side, the opposite wall was covered with climbing plants trained upon poles painted green and connected with crossway trellises. This lawn, this world of flowers, the gravelled paths, the simulated forest, the verdant palisades, were contained within the space of five and twenty square rods, which are worth to-day four hundred thousand francs,—the value of an actual forest. Here, in this solitude in the middle of Paris, the birds sang, thrushes, nightingales, warblers, bulfinches, and sparrows. The greenhouse was like an immense jardiniere, filling the air with perfume in winter as in summer. The means by which its atmosphere was made to order, torrid as in China or temperate as in Italy, were cleverly concealed. Pipes in which hot water circulated, or steam, were either hidden under ground or festooned with plants overhead. The boudoir was a large room. The miracle of the modern Parisian fairy named Architecture is to get all these many and great things out of a limited bit of ground.

The boudoir of the young countess was arranged to suit the taste of the artist to whom Comte Adam entrusted the decoration of the house. It is too full of pretty nothings to be a place for repose; one scarce knows where to sit down among carved Chinese work-tables with their myriads of fantastic figures inlaid in ivory, cups of yellow topaz mounted on filagree, mosaics which inspire theft, Dutch pictures in the style which Schinner has adopted, angels such as Steinbock conceived but often could not execute, statuettes modelled by genius pursued by creditors (the real explanation of the Arabian myth), superb sketches by our best artists, lids of chests made into panels alternating with fluted draperies of Italian silk, portieres hanging from rods of old oak in tapestried masses on which the figures of some hunting scene are swarming, pieces of furniture worthy to have belonged to Madame de

Pompadour, Persian rugs, et cetera. For a last graceful touch, all these elegant things were subdued by the half-light which filtered through embroidered curtains and added to their charm. On a table between the windows, among various curiosities, lay a whip, the handle designed by Mademoiselle de Fauveau, which proved that the countess rode on horseback.

Such is a lady's boudoir in 1837,—an exhibition of the contents of many shops, which amuse the eye, as if ennui were the one thing to be dreaded by the social world of the liveliest and most stirring capital in Europe. Why is there nothing of an inner life? nothing which leads to revery, nothing reposeful? Why indeed? Because no one in our day is sure of the future; we are living our lives like prodigal annuitants.

One morning Clementine appeared to be thinking of something. She was lying at full length on one of those marvellous couches from which it is almost impossible to rise, the upholsterer having invented them for lovers of the "far niente" and its attendant joys of laziness to sink into. The doors of the greenhouse were open, letting the odors of vegetation and the perfume of the tropics pervade the room. The young wife was looking at her husband who was smoking a narghile, the only form of pipe she would have suffered in that room. The portieres, held back by cords, gave a vista through two elegant salons, one white and gold, comparable only to that of the hotel Forbin-Janson, the other in the style of the Renaissance. The dining-room, which had no rival in Paris except that of the Baron de Nucingen, was at the end of a short gallery decorated in the manner of the middle-ages. This gallery opened on the side of the courtyard upon a large antechamber, through which could be seen the beauties of the staircase.

The count and countess had just finished breakfast; the sky was a sheet of azure without a cloud, April was nearly over. They had been married two years, and Clementine had just discovered for the first time that there was something resembling a secret or a mystery in her household. The Pole, let us say it to his honor, is usually helpless before a woman; he is so full of tenderness for her that in Poland he becomes her inferior, though Polish women make admirable wives. Now a Pole is still more easily vanquished by a Parisian woman. Consequently Comte Adam, pressed by questions, did not even attempt the innocent roguery of selling the suspected secret. It is always wise with a woman to get some good out of a mystery; she will like you the better for it, as a swindler respects an honest man the more when he finds he cannot swindle him. Brave in heart but not in speech, Comte Adam merely stipulated that he should not be compelled to answer until he had finished his narghile.

"If any difficulty occurred when we were travelling," said Clementine, "you always dismissed it by saying, 'Paz will settle that.' You never wrote to any one but Paz. When we returned here everybody kept saying, 'the captain, the captain.' If I want the carriage—'the captain.' Is there a bill to pay—'the captain.' If my horse is not properly bitted, they must speak to Captain Paz. In short, it is like a game of dominoes—Paz is everywhere. I hear of nothing but Paz, but I never see Paz. Who and what is Paz? Why don't you bring forth your Paz?"

"Isn't everything going on right?" asked the count, taking the "bocchettino" of his narghile from his lips.

"Everything is going on so right that other people with an income of two hundred thousand francs would ruin themselves by going at our pace, and we have only one hundred and ten thousand."

So saying she pulled the bell-cord (an exquisite bit of needlework). A footman entered, dressed like a minister.

"Tell Captain Paz that I wish to see him."

"If you think you are going to find out anything that way—" said Comte Adam, laughing.

It is well to mention that Adam and Clementine, married in December, 1835, had gone soon after the wedding to Italy, Switzerland, and Germany, where they spent the greater part of two years. Returning to Paris in November, 1837, the countess entered society for the first time as a married woman during the winter which had just ended, and she then became aware of the existence, half-suppressed and wholly dumb but very useful, of a species of factotum who was personally invisible, named Paz,—spelt thus, but pronounced "Patz."

"Monsieur le capitaine Paz begs Madame la comtesse to excuse him," said the footman, returning. "He is at the stables; as soon as he has changed his dress Comte Paz will present himself to Madame."

"What was he doing at the stables?"

"He was showing them how to groom Madame's horse," said the man. "He was not pleased with the way Constantin did it."

The countess looked at the footman. He was perfectly serious and did not add to his words the sort of smile by which servants usually comment on the actions of a superior who seems to them to derogate from his position.

"Ah! he was grooming Cora."

"Madame la comtesse intends to ride out this morning?" said the footman, leaving the room without further answer.

"Is Paz a Pole?" asked Clementine, turning to her husband, who nodded by way of affirmation.

Madame Laginska was silent, examining Adam. With her feet extended upon a cushion and her head poised like that of a bird on the edge of its nest listening to the noises in a grove, she would have seemed enchanting even to a blasé man. Fair and slender, and wearing her hair in curls, she was not unlike those semi-romantic pictures in the Keepsakes, especially when dressed, as she was this morning, in a breakfast gown of Persian silk, the folds of which could not disguise the beauty of her figure or the slimness of her waist. The silk with its brilliant colors being crossed upon the bosom showed the spring of the neck,—its whiteness contrasting delightfully against the tones of a guipure lace which lay upon her shoulders. Her eyes and their long black lashes added at this moment to the expression of curiosity which puckered her pretty mouth. On the forehead, which was well modelled, an observer would have noticed a roundness characteristic of the true Parisian woman,—self-willed, merry, well-informed, but inaccessible to vulgar seductions. Her hands, which were almost transparent, were hanging down at the end of each arm of her chair; the tapering fingers, slightly turned up at their points, showed nails like almonds, which caught the light. Adam smiled at his wife's impatience, and looked at her with a glance which two years of married life had not yet chilled. Already the little countess had made herself mistress of the situation, for she scarcely paid attention to her husband's admiration. In fact, in the look which she occasionally cast at him, there seemed to be the consciousness of a Frenchwoman's ascendancy over the puny, volatile, and red-haired Pole.

"Here comes Paz," said the count, hearing a step which echoed through the gallery.

The countess beheld a tall and handsome man, well-made, and bearing on his face the signs of pain which come of inward strength and secret endurance of sorrow. He wore one of those tight, frogged overcoats which were then called "polonaise." Thick, black hair, rather unkempt, covered his square head, and Clementine noticed his broad forehead shining like a block of white marble, for Paz held his visored cap in his hand. The hand itself was like that of the Infant Hercules. Robust health flourished on his face, which was divided by a large Roman nose and reminded Clementine of some handsome Transteverino. A black silk cravat added to the martial appearance of this six-foot mystery, with eyes of jet and Italian fervor. The amplitude of his pleated trousers, which allowed only the tips of his boots to be seen, revealed his faithfulness to the fashions of his own land. There was something really burlesque to a romantic woman in the striking contrast no one could fail to remark between the captain and the count, the little Pole with his pinched face and the stalwart soldier.

"Good morning, Adam," he said familiarly. Then he bowed courteously as he asked Clementine what he could do for her.

"You are Laginski's friend!" exclaimed the countess.

"For life and death," answered Paz, to whom the count threw a smile of affection as he drew a last puff from his perfumed pipe.

"Then why don't you take your meals with us? why did you not accompany us to Italy and Switzerland? why do you hide yourself in such a way that I am unable to thank you for the constant services that you do for us?" said the countess, with much vivacity of manner but no feeling.

In fact, she thought she perceived in Paz a sort of voluntary servitude. Such an idea carried with it in her mind a certain contempt for a social amphibian, a being half-secretary, half-bailiff, and yet neither the one nor the other, a poor relation, an embarrassing friend.

"Because, countess," he answered with perfect ease of manner, "there are no thanks due. I am Adam's friend, and it gives me pleasure to take care of his interests."

"And you remain standing for your pleasure, too," remarked Comte Adam.

Paz sat down on a chair near the door.

"I remember seeing you about the time I was married, and afterwards in the courtyard," said Clementine. "But why do you put yourself in a position of inferiority,—you, Adam's friend?"

"I am perfectly indifferent to the opinion of the Parisians," he replied. "I live for myself, or, if you like, for you two."

"But the opinion of the world as to a friend of my husband is not indifferent to me—"

"Ah, madame, the world will be satisfied if you tell them I am 'an original.'"

After a moment's silence he added, "Are you going out to-day?"

"Will you come with us to the Bois?"

"Certainly."

So saying, Paz bowed and withdrew.

"What a good soul he is!" said Adam. "He has all the simplicity of a child."

"Now tell me all about your relations with him," said Clementine.

"Paz, my dear," said Laginski, "belongs to a noble family as old and illustrious as our own. One of the Pazzi of Florence, at the time of their disasters, fled to Poland, where he settled with some of his property and founded the Paz family, to which the title of count was granted. This family, which distinguished itself greatly in the glorious days of our royal republic, became rich. The graft from the tree that was felled in Italy flourished so vigorously in Poland that there are several branches of the family still there. I need not tell you that some are rich and some are poor. Our Paz is the scion of a poor branch. He was an orphan, without other fortune than his sword, when he served in the regiment of the Grand Duke Constantine at the time of our revolution. Joining the Polish cause, he fought like a Pole, like a patriot, like a man who has nothing,—three good reasons for fighting well. In his last affair, thinking he was followed by his men, he dashed upon a Russian battery and was taken prisoner. I was there. His brave act roused me. 'Let us go and get him!' I said to my troop, and we charged the battery like a lot of foragers. I got Paz—I was the seventh man; we started twenty and came back eight, counting Paz. After Warsaw was sold we were forced to escape those Russians. By a curious chance, Paz and I happened to come together again, at the same hour and the same place, on the other side of the Vistula. I saw the poor captain arrested by some Prussians, who made themselves the blood-hounds of the Russians. When we have fished a man out of the Styx we cling to him. This new danger for poor Paz made me so unhappy that I let myself be taken too, thinking I could help him. Two men can get away where one will perish. Thanks to my name and some family connections in Prussia, the authorities shut their eyes to my escape. I got my dear captain through as a man of no consequence, a family servant, and we reached Dantzic. There we got on board a Dutch vessel and went to London. It took us two months to get there. My mother was ill in England, and expecting me. Paz and I took care of her till her death, which the Polish troubles hastened. Then we left London and came to France. Men who go through such adversities become like brothers. When I reached Paris, at twenty-two years of age, and found I had an income of over sixty thousand francs a year, without counting the proceeds of the diamonds and the pictures sold by my mother, I wanted to secure the future of my dear Paz before I launched into dissipation. I had often noticed the sadness in his eyes—sometimes tears were in them. I had had good reason to understand his soul, which is noble, grand, and generous to the core. I thought he might not like to be bound by benefits to a friend who was six years younger than himself, unless he could repay them. I was careless and frivolous, just as a young fellow is, and I knew I was certain to ruin myself at play, or get inveigled by some woman, and Paz and I might then be parted;

and though I had every intention of always looking out for him, I knew I might sometime or other forget to provide for him. In short, my dear angel, I wanted to spare him the pain and mortification of having to ask me for money, or of having to hunt me up if he got into distress. SO, one morning, after breakfast, when we were sitting with our feet on the andirons smoking pipes, I produced,—with the utmost precaution, for I saw him look at me uneasily,—a certificate of the Funds payable to bearer for a certain sum of money a year."

Clementine jumped up and went and seated herself on Adam's knee, put her arms round his neck, and kissed him. "Dear treasure!" she said, "how handsome he is! Well, what did Paz do?"

"Thaddeus turned pale," said the count, "but he didn't say a word."

"Oh! his name is Thaddeus, is it?"

"Yes; Thaddeus folded the paper and gave it back to me, and then he said: 'I thought, Adam, that we were one for life or death, and that we should never part. Do you want to be rid of me?' 'Oh!' I said, 'if you take it that way, Thaddeus, don't let us say another word about it. If I ruin myself you shall be ruined too.' 'You haven't fortune enough to live as a Laginski should,' he said, 'and you need a friend who will take care of your affairs, and be a father and a brother and a trusty confidant.' My dear child, as Paz said that he had in his look and voice, calm as they were, a maternal emotion, and also the gratitude of an Arab, the fidelity of a dog, the friendship of a savage,—not displayed, but ever ready. Faith! I seized him, as we Poles do, with a hand on each shoulder, and I kissed him on the lips. 'For life and death, then! all that I have is yours—do what you will with it.' It was he who found me this house and bought it for next to nothing. He sold my Funds high and bought in low, and we have paid for this barrack with the profits. He knows horses, and he manages to buy and sell at such advantage that my stable really costs very little; and yet I have the finest horses and the most elegant equipages in all Paris. Our servants, brave Polish soldiers chosen by him, would go through fire and water for us. I seem, as you say, to be ruining myself; and yet Paz keeps the house with such method and economy that he has even repaired some of my foolish losses at play,—the thoughtless folly of a young man. My dear, Thaddeus is as shrewd as two Genoese, as eager for gain as a Polish Jew, and provident as a good housekeeper. I never could force him to live as I did when I was a bachelor. Sometimes I had to use a sort of friendly coercion to make him go to the theatre with me when I was alone, or to the jovial little dinners I used to give at a tavern. He doesn't like social life."

"What does he like, then?" asked Clementine.

"Poland; he loves Poland and pines for it. His only spendings are sums he gives, more in my name than in his own, to some of our poor brother-exiles."

"Well, I shall love him, the fine fellow!" said the countess, "he looks to me as simple-hearted as he is grand."

"All these pretty things you have about you," continued Adam, who praised his friend in the noblest sincerity, "he picked up; he bought them at auction, or as bargains from the dealers. Oh! he's keener than they are themselves. If you see him rubbing his hands in the courtyard, you may be sure he has traded away one good horse for a better. He lives for me; his happiness is to see me elegant, in a perfectly appointed equipage. The duties he takes upon himself are all accomplished without fuss or emphasis. One evening I lost twenty thousand francs at whist. 'What will Paz say?' thought I as I walked home. Paz paid them to me, not without a sigh; but he never reproached me, even by a look. But that sigh of his restrained me more than the remonstrances of uncles, mothers, or wives could have done. 'Do you regret the money?' I said to him. 'Not for you or me, no,' he replied; 'but I was thinking that twenty poor Poles could have lived a year on that sum.' You must understand that the Pazzi are fully the equal of the Laginski, so I couldn't regard my dear Paz as an inferior. I never went out or came in without going first to Paz, as I would to my father. My fortune is his; and Thaddeus knows that if danger threatened him I would fling myself into it and drag him out, as I have done before."

"And that is saying a good deal, my dear friend," said the countess. "Devotion is like a flash of lightning. Men devote themselves in battle, but they no longer have the heart for it in Paris."

"Well," replied Adam, "I am always ready, as in battle, to devote myself to Paz. Our two characters have kept their natural asperities and defects, but the mutual comprehension of our souls has tightened the bond already close between us. It is quite possible to save a man's life and kill him afterwards if we find him a bad fellow; but Paz and I know THAT of each other which makes our friendship indissoluble. There's a constant exchange of happy thoughts and impressions between us; and really, perhaps, such a friendship as ours is richer than love."

A pretty hand closed the count's mouth so promptly that the action was somewhat like a blow.

"Yes," he said, "friendship, my dear angel, knows nothing of bankrupt sentiments and collapsed joys. Love, after giving more than it has, ends by giving less than it receives."

"One side as well as the other," remarked Clementine laughing.

"Yes," continued Adam, "whereas friendship only increases. You need not pucker up your lips at that, for we are, you and I, as much friends as lovers; we have, at least I hope so, combined the two sentiments in our happy marriage."

"I'll explain to you what it is that has made you and Thaddeus such good friends," said Clementine. "The difference in the lives you lead comes from your tastes and from necessity; from your likings, not your positions. As far as one can judge from merely seeing a man once, and also from what you tell me, there are times when the subaltern might become the superior."

"Oh, Paz is truly my superior," said Adam, naively; "I have no advantage over him except mere luck."

His wife kissed him for the generosity of those words.

"The extreme care with which he hides the grandeur of his feelings is one form of his superiority," continued the count. "I said to him once: 'You are a sly one; you have in your heart a vast domain within which you live and think.' He has a right to the title of count; but in Paris he won't be called anything but captain."

"The fact is that the Florentine of the middle-ages has reappeared in our century," said the countess. "Dante and Michael Angelo are in him."

"That's the very truth," cried Adam. "He is a poet in soul."

"So here I am, married to two Poles," said the young countess, with a gesture worthy of some genius of the stage.

"Dear child!" said Adam, pressing her to him, "it would have made me very unhappy if my friend did not please you. We were both rather afraid of it, he and I, though he was delighted at my marriage. You will make him very happy if you tell him that you love him,—yes, as an old friend."

"I'll go and dress, the day is so fine; and we will all three ride together," said Clementine, ringing for her maid.

II

Paz was leading so subterranean a life that the fashionable world of Paris asked who he was when the Comtesse Laginska was seen in the Bois de Boulogne riding between her husband and a stranger. During the ride Clementine insisted that Thaddeus should dine with them. This caprice of the sovereign lady compelled Paz to make an evening toilet. Clementine dressed for the occasion with a certain coquetry, in a style that impressed even Adam himself when she entered the salon where the two friends awaited her.

"Comte Paz," she said, "you must go with us to the Opera."

This was said in the tone which, coming from a woman means: "If you refuse we shall quarrel."

"Willingly, madame," replied the captain. "But as I have not the fortune of a count, have the kindness to call me captain."

"Very good, captain; give me your arm," she said,—taking it and leading the way to the dining-room with the flattering familiarity which enchants all lovers.

The countess placed the captain beside her; his behavior was that of a poor sub-lieutenant dining at his general's table. He let Clementine talk, listened deferentially as to a superior, did not differ with her in anything, and waited to be questioned before he spoke at all. He seemed actually stupid to the countess, whose coquettish little ways missed their mark in presence of such frigid gravity and conventional respect. In vain Adam kept saying: "Do be lively, Thaddeus; one would really suppose you were not at home. You must have made a wager to disconcert Clementine." Thaddeus continued heavy and half asleep. When the servants left the room at the end of the dessert the captain explained that his habits were diametrically opposite to those of society,—he went to bed at eight o'clock and got up very early in the morning; and he excused his dulness on the ground of being sleepy.

"My intention in taking you to the Opera was to amuse you, captain; but do as you prefer," said Clementine, rather piqued.

"I will go," said Paz.

"Duprez sings 'Guillaume Tell,'" remarked Adam. "But perhaps you would rather go to the 'Varietes'?"

The captain smiled and rang the bell. "Tell Constantin," he said to the footman, "to put the horses to the carriage instead of the coupe. We should be rather squeezed otherwise," he said to the count.

"A Frenchman would have forgotten that," remarked Clementine, smiling.

"Ah! but we are Florentines transplanted to the North," answered Thaddeus with a refinement of accent and a look in his eyes which made his conduct at table seem assumed for the occasion. There was too evident a contrast between his involuntary self-revelation in this speech and his behavior during dinner. Clementine examined the captain with a few of those covert glances which show a woman's surprise and also her capacity for observation.

It resulted from this little incident that silence reigned in the salon while the three took their coffee, a silence rather annoying to Adam, who was incapable of imagining the cause of it. Clementine no longer tried to draw out Thaddeus. The captain, on the other hand, retreated within his military stiffness and came out of it no more, neither on the way to the Opera nor in the box, where he seemed to be asleep.

"You see, madame, that I am a very stupid man," he said during the dance in the last act of "Guillaume Tell." "Am I not right to keep, as the saying is, to my own specialty?"

"In truth, my dear captain, you are neither a talker nor a man of the world, but you are perhaps Polish."

"Therefore leave me to look after your pleasures, your property, your household—it is all I am good for."

"Tartufe! pooh!" cried Adam, laughing. "My dear, he is full of ardor; he is thoroughly educated; he can, if he chooses, hold his own in any salon. Clementine, don't believe his modesty."

"Adieu, comtesse; I have obeyed your wishes so far; and now I will take the carriage and go home to bed and send it back for you."

Clementine bowed her head and let him go without replying.

"What a bear!" she said to the count. "You are a great deal nicer."

Adam pressed her hand when no one was looking.

"Poor, dear Thaddeus," he said, "he is trying to make himself disagreeable where most men would try to seem more amiable than I."

"Oh!" she said, "I am not sure but what there is some *calculation* in his behavior; he would have taken in an ordinary woman."

Half an hour later, when the chasseur, Boleslas, called out "Gate!" and the carriage was waiting for it to swing back, Clementine said to her husband, "Where does the captain perch?"

"Why, there!" replied Adam, pointing to a floor above the porte-cochere which had one window looking on the street. "His apartments are over the coachhouse."

"Who lives on the other side?" asked the countess.

"No one as yet," said Adam; "I mean that apartment for our children and their instructors."

"He didn't go to bed," said the countess, observing lights in Thaddeus's rooms when the carriage had passed under the portico supported by columns copied from those of the Tuileries, which replaced a vulgar zinc awning painted in stripes like cloth.

The captain, in his dressing-gown with a pipe in his mouth, was watching Clementine as she entered the vestibule. The day had been a hard one for him. And here is the reason why: A great and terrible emotion had taken possession of his heart on the day when Adam made him go to the Opera to see and give his opinion on Mademoiselle du Rouvre; and again when he saw her on the occasion of her marriage, and recognized in her the woman whom a man is forced to love exclusively. For this reason Paz strongly advised and promoted the long journey to Italy and elsewhere after the marriage. At peace so long as Clementine was away, his trial was renewed on the return of the happy household. As he sat at his window on this memorable night, smoking his latakia in a pipe of wild-cherry wood six feet long, given to him by Adam, these are the thoughts that were passing through his mind:—

"I, and God, who will reward me for suffering in silence, alone know how I love her! But how shall I manage to have neither her love nor her dislike?"

And his thoughts travelled far on this strange theme.

It must not be supposed that Thaddeus was living without pleasure, in the midst of his sufferings. The deceptions of this day, for instance, were a source of inward joy to him. Since the return of the count and countess he had daily felt ineffable satisfactions in knowing himself necessary to a household which, without his devotion to its interests, would infallibly have gone to ruin. What fortune can bear the strain of reckless prodigality? Clementine, brought up by a spendthrift father, knew nothing of the management of a household which the women of the present day, however rich or noble they are, are often compelled to undertake themselves. How few, in these days, keep a steward. Adam, on the other hand, son of one of the great Polish lords who let themselves be preyed on by the Jews, and are wholly incapable of managing even the wreck of their vast fortunes (for fortunes are vast in Poland), was not of a nature to check his own fancies or those of his wife. Left to himself he would probably have been ruined before his marriage. Paz had prevented him from gambling at the Bourse, and that says all.

Under these circumstances, Thaddeus, feeling that he loved Clementine in spite of himself, had not the resource of leaving the house and travelling in other lands to forget his passion. Gratitude, the key-note of his life, held him bound to that household where he alone could look after the affairs of the heedless owners. The long absence of Adam and Clementine had given him peace. But the countess had returned more lovely than ever, enjoying the freedom which marriage brings to a Parisian woman, displaying the graces of a young wife and the nameless attraction she gains from the happiness, or the independence, bestowed upon her by a young man as trustful, as chivalric, and as much in love as Adam. To know that he was the pivot on which the splendor the household depended, to see Clementine when she got out of her carriage on returning from some fete, or got into it in the morning when she took her drive, to meet her on the boulevards in her pretty equipage, looking like a flower in a whorl of leaves, inspired poor Thaddeus with mysterious delights, which glowed in the depths of his heart but gave no signs upon his face.

How happened it that for five whole months the countess had never perceived the captain? Because he hid himself from her knowledge, and carefully concealed the pains he took to avoid her. Nothing so resembles the Divine love as hopeless human love. A man must have great depth of heart to devote himself in silence and obscurity to a woman. In such a heart is the worship of love for love's sake only—sublime avarice, sublime because ever generous and founded on the mysterious existence of the principles of creation. *Effect* is nature, and nature is enchanting; it belongs to man, to the poet, the painter, the lover. But *Cause*, to a few privileged souls and to certain mighty thinkers, is superior to nature. Cause is God. In the sphere of causes live the Newtons and all such thinkers as Laplace, Kepler, Descartes, Malebranche, Spinoza, Buffon; also the true poets and solitarys of the second Christian century, and the Saint Teresas of Spain, and such sublime ecstatics. All human sentiments bear analogy to these conditions whenever the mind abandons Effect for Cause. Thaddeus had reached this height, at which all things change their relative aspect. Filled with the joys unutterable of a creator he had attained in his love to all that genius has revealed to us of grandeur.

"No," he was thinking to himself as he watched the curling smoke of his pipe, "she was not entirely deceived. She might break up my friendship with Adam if she took a dislike to me; but if she coquetted with me to amuse herself, what would become of me?"

The conceit of this last supposition was so foreign to the modest nature and

Teutonic timidity of the captain that he scolded himself for admitting it, and went to bed, resolved to await events before deciding on a course.

The next day Clementine breakfasted very contentedly without Paz, and without even noticing his disobedience to her orders. It happened to be her reception day, when the house was thrown open with a splendor that was semi-royal. She paid no attention to the absence of Comte Paz, on whom all the burden of these parade days fell.

"Good!" thought he, as he heard the last carriages driving away at two in the morning; "it was only the caprice or the curiosity of a Parisian woman that made her want to see me."

After that the captain went back to his ordinary habits and ways, which had been somewhat upset by this incident. Diverted by her Parisian occupations, Clementine appeared to have forgotten Paz. It must not be thought an easy matter to reign a queen over fickle Paris. Does any one suppose that fortunes alone are risked in the great game? The winters are to fashionable women what a campaign once was to the soldiers of the Empire. What works of art and genius are expended on a gown or a garland in which to make a sensation! A fragile, delicate creature will wear her stiff and brilliant harness of flowers and diamonds, silk and steel, from nine at night till two and often three o'clock in the morning. She eats little, to attract remark to her slender waist; she satisfied her hunger with debilitating tea, sugared cakes, ices which heat her, or slices of heavy pastry. The stomach is made to yield to the orders of coquetry. The awakening comes too late. A fashionable woman's whole life is in contradiction to the laws of nature, and nature is pitiless. She has no sooner risen than she makes an elaborate morning toilet, and thinks of the one which she means to wear in the afternoon. The moment she is dressed she has to receive and make visits, and go to the Bois either on horseback or in a carriage. She must practise the art of smiling, and must keep her mind on the stretch to invent new compliments which shall seem neither common nor far-fetched. All women do not succeed in this. It is no surprise, therefore, to find a young woman who entered fashionable society fresh and healthy, faded and worn out at the end of three years. Six months spent in the country will hardly heal the wounds of the winter. We hear continually, in these days, of mysterious ailments,—gastritis, and so forth,—ills unknown to women when they busied themselves about their households. In the olden time women only appeared in the world at intervals; now they are always on the scene. Clementine found she had to struggle for her supremacy. She was cited, and that alone brought jealousies; and the care and watchfulness exacted by this contest with her rivals left little time even to love her husband. Paz might well be forgotten. Nevertheless, in the month of May, as she drove home from the

Bois, just before she left Paris for Ronquerolles, her uncle's estate in Burgundy, she noticed Thaddeus, elegantly dressed, sauntering on one of the side-paths of the Champs-Elysees, in the seventh heaven of delight at seeing his beautiful countess in her elegant carriage with its spirited horses and sparkling liveries,—in short, his beloved family the admired of all.

"There's the captain," she said to her husband.

"He's happy!" said Adam. "This is his delight. He knows there's no equipage more elegant than ours, and he is rejoicing to think that some people envy it. Have you only just noticed him? I see him there nearly every day."

"I wonder what he is thinking about now," said Clementine.

"He is thinking that this winter has cost a good deal, and that it is time we went to economize with your old uncle Ronquerolles," replied Adam.

The countess stopped the carriage near Paz, and bade him take the seat beside her. Thaddeus grew as red as a cherry.

"I shall poison you," he said; "I have been smoking."

"Doesn't Adam poison me?" she said.

"Yes, but he is Adam," returned the captain.

"And why can't Thaddeus have the same privileges?" asked the countess, smiling.

That divine smile had a power which triumphed over the heroic resolutions of poor Paz; he looked at Clementine with all the fire of his soul in his eyes, though, even so, its flame was tempered by the angelic gratitude of the man whose life was based upon that virtue. The countess folded her arms in her shawl, lay back pensively on her cushions, ruffling the feathers of her pretty bonnet, and looked at the people who passed her. That flash of a great and hitherto resigned soul reached her sensibilities. What was Adam's merit in her eyes? It was natural enough to have courage and generosity. But Thaddeus— surely Thaddeus possessed, or seemed to possess, some great superiority over Adam. They were dangerous thoughts which took possession of the countess's mind as she again noticed the contrast of the fine presence that distinguished Thaddeus, and the puny frame in which Adam showed the degenerating effects of intermarriage among the Polish aristocratic families. The devil alone knew the thoughts that were in Clementine's head, for she sat still, with thoughtful, dreamy eyes, and without saying a word until they reached home.

"You will dine with us; I shall be angry if you disobey me," she said as the carriage turned in. "You are Thaddeus to me, as you are to Adam. I know your obligations to him, but I also know those we are under to you. Both generosities are natural—but you are generous every day and all day. My father dines here to-day, also my uncle Ronquerolles and my aunt Madame de Serizy. Dress yourself therefore," she said, taking the hand he offered to assist her from the carriage.

Thaddeus went to his own room to dress with a joyful heart, though shaken by an inward dread. He went down at the last moment and behaved through dinner as he had done on the first occasion, that is, like a soldier fit only for his duties as a steward. But this time Clementine was not his dupe; his glance had enlightened her. The Marquis de Ronquerolles, one of the ablest diplomates after Talleyrand, who had served with de Marsay during his short ministry, had been informed by his niece of the real worth and character of Comte Paz, and knew how modestly he made himself the steward of his friend Laginski.

"And why is this the first time I have the pleasure of seeing Comte Paz?" asked the marquis.

"Because he is so shy and retiring," replied Clementine with a look at Paz telling him to change his behavior.

Alas! that we should have to avow it, at the risk of rendering the captain less interesting, but Paz, though superior to his friend Adam, was not a man of parts. His apparent superiority was due to his misfortunes. In his lonely and poverty-stricken life in Warsaw he had read and taught himself a good deal; he had compared and meditated. But the gift of original thought which makes a great man he did not possess, and it can never be acquired. Paz, great in heart only, approached in heart to the sublime; but in the sphere of sentiments, being more a man of action than of thought, he kept his thoughts to himself; and they only served therefore to eat his heart out. What, after all, is a thought unexpressed?

After Clementine's little speech, the Marquis de Ronquerolles and his sister exchanged a singular glance, embracing their niece, Comte Adam, and Paz. It was one of those rapid scenes which take place only in France and Italy,—the two regions of the world (all courts excepted) where eyes can say everything. To communicate to the eye the full power of the soul, to give it the value of speech, needs either the pressure of extreme servitude, or complete liberty. Adam, the Marquis du Rouvre, and Clementine did not observe this luminous by-play of the old coquette and the old diplomatist, but Paz, the faithful watchdog, understood its meaning. It was, we must remark, an affair of two seconds; but to describe the tempest it roused in the captain's soul would take far too much space in this brief history.

"What!" he said to himself, "do the aunt and uncle think I might be loved? Then my happiness only depends on my own audacity! But Adam—"

Ideal love and desire clashed with gratitude and friendship, all equally powerful, and, for a moment, love prevailed. The lover would have his day. Paz became brilliant, he tried to please, he told the story of the Polish insurrection in noble words, being questioned about it by the diplomatist. By the end of dinner Paz saw Clementine hanging upon his lips and regarding him as a hero, forgetting that Adam too, after sacrificing a third of his vast fortune, had been an exile. At nine o'clock, after coffee had been served, Madame de Serizy kissed her niece on the forehead, pressed her hand, and went away, taking Adam with her and leaving the Marquis de Ronquerolles and the Marquis du Rouvre, who soon followed. Paz and Clementine were alone together.

"I will leave you now, madame," said Thaddeus. "You will of course rejoin them at the Opera?"

"No," she answered, "I don't like dancing, and they give an odious ballet to-night 'La Revolte au Serail.'"

There was a moment's silence.

"Two years ago Adam would not have gone to the Opera without me," said Clementine, not looking at Paz.

"He loves you madly," replied Thaddeus.

"Yes, and because he loves me madly he is all the more likely not to love me to-morrow," said the countess.

"How inexplicable Parisian women are!" exclaimed Thaddeus. "When they are loved to madness they want to be loved reasonably: and when they are loved reasonably they reproach a man for not loving them at all."

"And they are quite right. Thaddeus," she went on, smiling, "I know Adam well; I am not angry with him; he is volatile and above all grand seigneur. He will always be content to have me as his wife and he will never oppose any of my tastes, but—"

"Where is the marriage in which there are no 'buts'?" said Thaddeus, gently, trying to give another direction to Clementine's mind.

The least presuming of men might well have had the thought which came near rendering this poor lover beside himself; it was this: "If I do not tell her now that I love her I am a fool," he kept saying to himself.

Neither spoke; and there came between the pair one of those deep silences that are crowded with thoughts. The countess examined Paz covertly, and Paz observed her in a mirror. Buried in an armchair like a man digesting his dinner, the image of a husband or an indifferent old man, Paz crossed his hands upon his stomach and twirled his thumbs mechanically, looking stupidly at them.

"Why don't you tell me something good of Adam?" cried Clementine suddenly. "Tell me that he is not volatile, you who know him so well."

The cry was fine.

"Now is the time," thought poor Paz, "to put an insurmountable barrier between us. Tell you good of Adam?" he said aloud. "I love him; you would not believe me; and I am incapable of telling you harm. My position is very difficult between you."

Clementine lowered her head and looked down at the tips of his varnished boots.

"You Northern men have nothing but physical courage," she said complainingly; "you have no constancy in your opinions."

"How will you amuse yourself alone, madame?" said Paz, assuming a careless air.

"Are not you going to keep me company?"

"Excuse me for leaving you."

"What do you mean? Where are you going?"

The thought of a heroic falsehood had come into his head.

"I—I am going to the Circus in the Champs Elysees; it opens to-night, and I can't miss it."

"Why not?" said Clementine, questioning him by a look that was half-anger.

"Must I tell you why?" he said, coloring; "must I confide to you what I hide from Adam, who thinks my only love is Poland."

"Ah! a secret in our noble captain?"

"A disgraceful one—which you will perhaps understand, and pity."

"You, disgraced?"

"Yes, I, Comte Paz; I am madly in love with a girl who travels all over France with the Bouthor family,—people who have the rival circus to Franconi; but they play only at fairs. I have made the director at the Cirque-Olympique engage her."

"Is she handsome?"

"To my thinking," said Paz, in a melancholy tone. "Malaga (that's her stage name) is strong, active, and supple. Why do I prefer her to all other women in the world?—well, I can't tell you. When I look at her, with her black hair tied with a blue satin ribbon, floating on her bare and olive-colored shoulders, and when she is dressed in a white tunic with a gold edge, and a knitted silk bodice that makes her look like a living Greek statue, and when I see her carrying those flags in her hand to the sound of martial music, and jumping through the paper hoops which tear as she goes through, and lighting so gracefully on the galloping horse to such applause,—no hired clapping,— well, all that moves me."

"More than a handsome woman in a ballroom?" asked Clementine, with amazement and curiosity.

"Yes," answered Paz, in a choking voice. "Such agility, such grace under constant danger seems to me the height of triumph for a woman. Yes, madame, Cinti and Malibran, Grisi and Taglioni, Pasta and Ellsler, all who reign or have reigned on the stage, can't be compared, to my mind, with Malaga, who can jump on or off a horse at full gallop, or stand on the point of one foot and fall easily into the saddle, and knit stockings, break eggs, and make an omelette with the horse at full speed, to the admiration of the people, —the real people, peasants and soldiers. Malaga, madame, is dexterity personified; her little wrist or her little foot can rid her of three or four men. She is the goddess of gymnastics."

"She must be stupid—"

"Oh, no," said Paz, "I find her as amusing as the heroine of 'Peveril of the Peak.' Thoughtless as a Bohemian, she says everything that comes into her head; she thinks no more about the future than you do of the sous you fling to the poor. She says grand things sometimes. You couldn't make her believe that an old diplomatist was a handsome young man, not if you offered her a million of francs. Such love as hers is perpetual flattery to a man. Her health is positively insolent, and she has thirty-two oriental pearls in lips of coral. Her muzzle—that's what she calls the lower part of her face—has, as Shakespeare expresses it, the savor of a heifer's nose. She can make a man unhappy. She likes handsome men, strong men, Alexanders, gymnasts, clowns. Her trainer, a horrible brute, used to beat her to make her supple, and graceful, and intrepid—"

"You are positively intoxicated with Malaga."

"Oh, she is called Malaga only on the posters," said Paz, with a piqued air. "She lives in the rue Saint-Lazare, in a pretty apartment on the third story, all velvet and silk, like a princess. She has two lives, her circus life and the life of a pretty woman."

"Does she love you?"

"She loves me—now you will laugh—solely because I'm a Pole. She saw an engraving of Poles rushing with Poniatowski into the Elster,—for all France persists in thinking that the Elster, where it is impossible to get drowned, is an impetuous flood, in which Poniatowski and his followers were engulfed. But in the midst of all this I am very unhappy, madame."

A tear of rage fell from his eyes and affected the countess.

"You men have such a passion for singularity."

"And you?" said Thaddeus.

"I know Adam so well that I am certain he could forget me for some mountebank like your Malaga. Where did you first see her?"

"At Saint-Cloud, last September, on the fete-day. She was at a corner of a booth covered with flags, where the shows are given. Her comrades, all in Polish costumes, were making a horrible racket. I watched her standing there, silent and dumb, and I thought I saw a melancholy expression in her face; in truth there was enough about her to sadden a girl of twenty. That touched me."

The countess was sitting in a delicious attitude, pensive and rather melancholy.

"Poor, poor Thaddeus!" she exclaimed. Then, with the kindliness of a true great lady she added, not without a malicious smile, "Well go, go to your Circus."

Thaddeus took her hand, kissed it, leaving a hot tear upon it, and went out.

Having invented this passion for a circus-rider, he bethought him that he must give it some reality. The only truth in his tale was the momentary attention he had given to Malaga at Saint-Cloud; and he had since seen her name on the posters of the Circus, where the clown, for a tip of five francs, had told him that the girl was a foundling, stolen perhaps. Thaddeus now went to the Circus and saw her again. For ten francs one of the grooms (who take the place in circuses of the dressers at a theatre) informed him that Malaga was named Marguerite Turquet, and lived on the fifth story of a house in the rue des Fosses-du-Temple.

The following day Paz went to the faubourg du Temple, found the house, and asked to see Mademoiselle Turquet, who during the summer was substituting for the leading horsewoman at the Cirque-Olympique, and a supernumerary at a boulevard theatre in winter.

"Malaga!" cried the portress, rushing into the attic, "there's a fine gentleman wanting you. He is getting information from Chapuzot, who is playing him off to give me time to tell you."

"Thank you, M'ame Chapuzot; but what will he think of me if he finds me ironing my gown?"

"Pooh! when a man's in love he loves everything about us."

"Is he an Englishman? they are fond of horses."

"No, he looks to me Spanish."

"That's a pity; they say Spaniards are always poor. Stay here with me, M'ame Chapuzot; I don't want him to think I'm deserted."

"Who is it you are looking for, monsieur?" asked Madame Chapuzot, opening the door for Thaddeus, who had now come upstairs.

"Mademoiselle Turquet."

"My dear," said the portress, with an air of importance, "here is some one to see you."

A line on which the clothes were drying caught the captain's hat and knocked it off.

"What is it you wish, monsieur?" said Malaga, picking up the hat and giving it to him.

"I saw you at the Circus," said Thaddeus, "and you reminded me of a daughter whom I have lost, mademoiselle; and out of affection for my Heloise, whom you resemble in a most striking manner, I should like to be of some service to you, if you will permit me."

"Why, certainly; pray sit down, general," said Madame Chapuzot; "nothing could be more straightforward, more gallant."

"But I am not gallant, my good lady," exclaimed Paz. "I am an unfortunate father who tries to deceive himself by a resemblance."

"Then am I to pass for your daughter?" said Malaga, slyly, and not in the least suspecting the perfect sincerity of his proposal.

"Yes," said Paz, "and I'll come and see you sometimes. But you shall be lodged in better rooms, comfortably furnished."

"I shall have furniture!" cried Malaga, looking at Madame Chapuzot.

"And servants," said Paz, "and all you want."

Malaga looked at the stranger suspiciously.

"What countryman is monsieur?"

"I am a Pole."

"Oh! then I accept," she said.

Paz departed, promising to return.

"Well, that's a stiff one!" said Marguerite Turquet, looking at Madame Chapuzot; "I'm half afraid he is wheedling me, to carry out some fancy of his own—Pooh! I'll risk it."

A month after this eccentric interview the circus-rider was living in a comfortable apartment furnished by Comte Adam's own upholsterer, Paz having judged it desirable to have his folly talked about at the hotel Laginski. Malaga, to whom this adventure was like a leaf out of the Arabian Nights, was served by Monsieur and Madame Chapuzot in the double capacity of friends and servants. The Chapuzots and Marguerite were constantly expecting some result of all this; but at the end of three months none of them were able to make out the meaning of the Polish count's caprice. Paz arrived duly and passed about an hour there once a week, during which time he sat in the salon, and never went into Malaga's boudoir nor into her bedroom, in spite of the clever manoeuvring of the Chapuzots and Malaga to get him there. The count would ask questions as to the small events of Marguerite's life, and each time that he came he left two gold pieces of forty francs each on the mantel-piece.

"He looks as if he didn't care to be here," said Madame Chapuzot.

"Yes," said Malaga, "the man's as cold as an icicle."

"But he's a good fellow all the same," cried Chapuzot, who was happy in a new suit of clothes made of blue cloth, in which he looked like the servant of some minister.

The sum which Paz deposited weekly on the mantel-piece, joined to Malaga's meagre salary, gave her the means of sumptuous living compared with her former poverty. Wonderful stories went the rounds of the Circus about Malaga's good-luck. Her vanity increased the six thousand francs which Paz had spent on her furniture to sixty thousand. According to the clowns and the supers, Malaga was squandering money; and she now appeared at the Circus wearing burnous and shawls and elegant scarfs. The Pole, it was agreed on all sides, was the best sort of man a circus-rider had ever encountered, not fault-finding nor jealous, and willing to let Malaga do just what she liked.

"Some women have the luck of it," said Malaga's rival, "and I'm not one of them,—though I do draw a third of the receipts."

Malaga wore pretty things, and occasionally "showed her head" (a term in the lexicon of such characters) in the Bois, where the fashionable young men of the day began to remark her. In fact, before long Malaga was very much talked about in the questionable world of equivocal women, who presently attacked her good fortune by calumnies. They said she was a somnambulist, and the Pole was a magnetizer who was using her to discover the philosopher's stone. Some even more envenomed scandals drove her to a curiosity that was greater than Psyche's. She reported them in tears to Paz.

"When I want to injure a woman," she said in conclusion, "I don't calumniate her; I don't declare that some one magnetizes her to get stones out of her, but I say plainly that she is humpbacked, and I prove it. Why do you compromise me in this way?"

Paz maintained a cruel silence. Madame Chapuzot was not long in discovering the name and title of Comte Paz; then she heard certain positive facts at the hotel Laginski: for instance, that Paz was a bachelor, and had never been known to have a daughter, alive or dead, in Poland or in France. After that Malaga could not control a feeling of terror.

"My dear child," Madame Chapuzot would say, "that monster—" (a man who contented himself with only looking, in a sly way,—not daring to come out and say things,—and such a beautiful creature too, as Malaga,—of course such a man was a monster, according to Madame Chapuzot's ideas) "—that monster is trying to get a hold upon you, and make you do something illegal and criminal. Holy Father, if you should get into the police-courts! it makes me tremble from head to foot; suppose they should put you in the newspapers! I'll tell you what I should do in your place; I'd warn the police."

One particular day, after many foolish notions had fermented for sometime in Malaga's mind, Paz having laid his money as usual on the mantel-piece, she seized the bits of gold and flung them in his face, crying out, "I don't want stolen money!"

The captain gave the gold to Chapuzot, went away without a word, and did not return.

Clementine was at this time at her uncle's place in Burgundy.

When the Circus troop discovered that Malaga had lost her Polish count, much excitement was produced among them. Malaga's display of honor was considered folly by some, and shrewdness by others. The conduct of the Pole, however, even when discussed by the cleverest of women, seemed inexplicable. Thaddeus received in the course of the next week thirty-seven letters from women of their kind. Happily for him, his astonishing reserve did not excite the curiosity of the fashionable world, and was only discussed in the demi-mondaine regions.

Two weeks later the handsome circus-rider, crippled by debt, wrote the following letter to Comte Paz, which, having fallen into the hands of Comte Adam, was read by several of the dandies of the day, who pronounced it a masterpiece:—

"You, whom I still dare to call my friend, will you not pity me after all that has passed,—which you have so ill understood? My heart disavows whatever may have wounded your feelings. If I was fortunate enough to charm you and keep you beside me in the past, return to me; otherwise, I shall fall into despair. Poverty has overtaken me, and you do not know what *horrid things* it brings with it. Yesterday I lived on a herring at two sous, and one sou of bread. Is that a breakfast for the woman you loved? The Chapuzots have left me, though they seemed so devoted. Your desertion has caused me to see to the bottom of all human attachments. The dog we feed does not leave us, but the Chapuzots have gone. A sheriff has seized everything on behalf of the landlord, who has no heart, and the jeweller, who refused to wait even ten days,—for when we lose the confidence of such as you, credit goes too. What a position for women who have nothing to reproach themselves with but the happiness they have given! My friend, I have taken all I have of any value to *my uncle's;* I have nothing but the memory of you left, and here is the winter coming on. I shall be fireless when it turns cold; for the boulevards are to play only melodramas, in which I have nothing but little bits of parts which don't *pose* a woman. How could you misunderstand the nobleness of my feelings for you?—for there are two ways of expressing gratitude. You who seemed so happy in seeing me well-off, how can you leave me in poverty? Oh, my sole friend on

31

earth, before I go back to the country fairs with Bouthor's circus,
where I can at least make a living, forgive me if I wish to know
whether I have lost you forever. If I were to let myself think of
you when I jump through the hoops, I should be sure to break my legs
by losing *a time*. Whatever may be the result, I am yours for life.

"Marguerite Turquet."

"That letter," thought Thaddeus, shouting with laughter, "is worth the ten thousand francs I have spent upon her."

III

Clementine came home the next day, and the day after that Paz beheld her again, more beautiful and graceful than ever. After dinner, during which the countess treated Paz with an air of perfect indifference, a little scene took place in the salon between the count and his wife when Thaddeus had left them. On pretence of asking Adam's advice, Thaddeus had left Malaga's letter with him, as if by mistake.

"Poor Thaddeus!" said Adam, as Paz disappeared, "what a misfortune for a man of his distinction to be the plaything of the lowest kind of circus-rider. He will lose everything, and get lower and lower, and won't be recognizable before long. Here, read that," added the count, giving Malaga's letter to his wife.

Clementine read the letter, which smelt of tobacco, and threw it from her with a look of disgust.

"Thick as the bandage is over his eyes," continued Adam, "he must have found out something; Malaga tricked him, no doubt."

"But he goes back to her," said Clementine, "and he will forgive her! It is for such horrible women as that that you men have indulgence."

"Well, they need it," said Adam.

"Thaddeus used to show some decency—in living apart from us," she remarked. "He had better go altogether."

"Oh, my dear angel, that's going too far," said the count, who did not want the death of the sinner.

Paz, who knew Adam thoroughly, had enjoined him to secrecy, pretending to excuse his dissipations, and had asked his friend to lend him a few thousand francs for Malaga.

"He is a very firm fellow," said Adam.

"How so?" asked Clementine.

"Why, for having spent no more than ten thousand francs on her, and letting her send him that letter before he would ask me for enough to pay her debts. For a Pole, I call that firm."

"He will ruin you," said Clementine, in the sharp tone of a Parisian woman, when she shows her feline distrusts.

"Oh, I know him," said Adam; "he will sacrifice Malaga, if I ask him."

"We shall see," remarked the countess.

"If it is best for his own happiness, I sha'n't hesitate to ask him to leave her. Constantin says that since Paz has been with her he, sober as he is, has sometimes come home quite excited. If he takes to intoxication I shall be just as grieved as if he were my own son."

"Don't tell me anything more about it," cried the countess, with a gesture of disgust.

Two days later the captain perceived in the manner, the tones of voice, but, above all, in the eyes of the countess, the terrible results of Adam's confidences. Contempt had opened a gulf between the beloved woman and himself. He was suddenly plunged into the deepest distress of mind, for the thought gnawed him, "I have myself made her despise me!" His own folly stared him in the face. Life then became a burden to him, the very sun turned gray. And yet, amid all these bitter thoughts, he found again some moments of pure joy. There were times when he could give himself up wholly to his admiration for his mistress, who paid not the slightest attention to him. Hanging about in corners at her parties and receptions, silent, all heart and eyes, he never lost one of her attitudes, nor a tone of her voice when she sang. He lived in her life; he groomed the horse which *she* rode, he studied the ways and means of that splendid establishment, to the interests of which he was now more devoted than ever. These silent pleasures were buried in his heart like those of a mother, whose heart a child never knows; for is it knowing anything unless we know it all? His love was more perfect than the love of Petrarch for Laura, which found its ultimate reward in the treasures of fame, the triumph of the poem which she had inspired. Surely the emotion that the Chevalier d'Assas felt in dying must have been to him a lifetime of joy. Such emotions as these Paz enjoyed daily,—without dying, but also without the guerdon of immortality.

But what is Love, that, in spite of all these ineffable delights, Paz should still have been unhappy? The Catholic religion has so magnified Love that she has wedded it indissolubly to respect and nobility of spirit. Love is therefore attended by those sentiments and qualities of which mankind is proud; it is rare to find true Love existing where contempt is felt. Thaddeus was suffering from the wounds his own hand had given him. The trial of his former life, when he lived beside his mistress, unknown, unappreciated, but generously working for her, was better than this. Yes, he wanted the reward of his virtue, her respect, and he had lost it. He grew thin and yellow, and so ill with constant low fever that during the month of January he was obliged to keep his bed, though he refused to see a doctor. Comte Adam became very uneasy about him; but the countess had the cruelty to remark: "Let him alone; don't you see it is only some Olympian trouble?" This remark, being repeated to Thaddeus, gave him the courage of despair; he left his bed, went out, tried a few amusements, and recovered his health.

About the end of February Adam lost a large sum of money at the Jockey-Club, and as he was afraid of his wife, he begged Thaddeus to let the sum appear in the accounts as if he had spent it on Malaga.

"There's nothing surprising in your spending that sum on the girl; but if the countess finds out that I have lost it at cards I shall be lowered in her opinion, and she will always be suspicious in future."

"Ha! this, too!" exclaimed Thaddeus, with a sigh.

"Now, Thaddeus, if you will do me this service we shall be forever quits,— though, indeed, I am your debtor now."

"Adam, you will have children; don't gamble any more," said Paz.

"So Malaga has cost us another twenty thousand francs," cried the countess, some time later, when she discovered this new generosity to Paz. "First, ten thousand, now twenty more,—thirty thousand! the income of which is fifteen hundred! the cost of my box at the Opera, and the whole fortune of many a bourgeois. Oh, you Poles!" she said, gathering some flowers in her greenhouse; "you are really incomprehensible. Why are you not furious with him?"

"Poor Paz is—"

"Poor Paz, poor Paz, indeed!" she cried, interrupting him, "what good does he do us? I shall take the management of the household myself. You can give him the allowance he refused, and let him settle it as he likes with his Circus."

"He is very useful to us, Clementine. He has certainly saved over forty thousand francs this last year. And besides, my dear angel, he has managed to put a hundred thousand with Nucingen, which a steward would have pocketed."

Clementine softened down; but she was none the less hard in her feelings to Thaddeus. A few days later, she requested him to come to that boudoir where, one year earlier, she had been surprised into comparing him with her husband. This time she received him alone, without perceiving the slightest danger in so doing.

"My dear Paz," she said, with the condescending familiarity of the great to their inferiors, "if you love Adam as you say you do, you will do a thing which he will not ask of you, but which I, his wife, do not hesitate to exact."

"About Malaga?" said Thaddeus, with bitterness in his heart.

"Well, yes," she said; "if you wish to end your days in this house and continue good friends with us, you must give her up. How an old soldier—"

"I am only thirty-five, and haven't a white hair."

"You look old," she said, "and that's the same thing. How so careful a manager, so distinguished a—"

The horrible part of all this was her evident intention to rouse a sense of honor in his soul which she thought extinct.

"—so distinguished a man as you are, Thaddeus," she resumed after a momentary pause which a gesture of his hand had led her to make, "can allow yourself to be caught like a boy! Your proceedings have made that woman celebrated. My uncle wanted to see her, and he did see her. My uncle is not the only one; Malaga receives a great many gentlemen. I did think you such a noble soul. For shame! Will she be such a loss that you can't replace her?"

"Madame, if I knew any sacrifice I could make to recover your esteem I would make it; but to give up Malaga is not one—"

"In your position, that is what I should say myself, if I were a man," replied Clementine. "Well, if I accept it as a great sacrifice there can be no ill-will between us."

Paz left the room, fearing he might commit some great folly, and feeling that wild ideas were getting the better of him. He went to walk in the open air, lightly dressed in spite of the cold, but without being able to cool the fire in his cheeks or on his brow.

"I thought you had a noble soul,"—the words still rang in his ears.

"A year ago," he said to himself, "she thought me a hero who could fight the Russians single-handed!"

He thought of leaving the hotel Laginski, and taking service with the spahis and getting killed in Africa, but the same great fear checked him. "Without me," he thought, "what would become of them? they would soon be ruined. Poor countess! what a horrible life it would be for her if she were reduced to even thirty thousand francs a year. No, since all is lost for me in this world,— courage! I will keep on as I am."

Every one knows that since 1830 the carnival in Paris has undergone a transformation which has made it European, and far more burlesque and otherwise lively than the late Carnival of Venice. Is it that the diminishing fortunes of the present time have led Parisians to invent a way of amusing themselves collectively, as for instance at their clubs, where they hold salons without hostesses and without manners, but very cheaply? However this may be, the month of March was prodigal of balls, at which dancing, joking, coarse fun, excitement, grotesque figures, and the sharp satire of Parisian wit, produced extravagant effects. These carnival follies had their special Pandemonium in the rue Saint-Honore and their Napoleon in Musard, a small man born expressly to lead an orchestra as noisy as the disorderly audience, and to set the time for the galop, that witches' dance, which was one of Auber's triumphs, for it did not really take form or poesy till the grand galop in "Gustave" was given to the world. That tremendous finale might serve as the symbol of an epoch in which for the last fifty years all things have hurried by with the rapidity of a dream.

Now, it happened that the grave Thaddeus, with one divine and immaculate image in his heart, proposed to Malaga, the queen of the carnival dances, to spend an evening at the Musard ball; because he knew the countess, disguised to the teeth, intended to come there with two friends, all three accompanied by their husbands, and look on at the curious spectacle of one of these crowded balls.

On Shrove Tuesday, of the year 1838, at four o'clock in the morning, the countess, wrapped in a black domino and sitting on the lower step of the platform in the Babylonian hall, where Valentino has since then given his concerts, beheld Thaddeus, as Robert Macaire, threading the galop with Malaga in the dress of a savage, her head garnished with plumes like the horse of a hearse, and bounding through the crowd like a will-o-the-wisp.

"Ah!" said Clementine to her husband, "you Poles have no honor at all! I did believe in Thaddeus. He gave me his word that he would leave that woman; he did not know that I should be here, seeing all unseen."

A few days later she requested Paz to dine with them. After dinner Adam left them alone together, and Clementine reproved Paz and let him know very plainly that she did not wish him to live in her house any longer.

"Yes, madame," said Paz, humbly, "you are right; I am a wretch; I did give you my word. But you see how it is; I put off leaving Malaga till after the carnival. Besides, that woman exerts an influence over me which——"

"An influence!—a woman who ought to be turned out of Musard's by the police for such dancing!"

"I agree to all that; I accept the condemnation and I'll leave your house. But you know Adam. If I give up the management of your property you must show energy yourself. I may have been to blame about Malaga, but I have taken the whole charge of your affairs, managed your servants, and looked after the very least details. I cannot leave you until I see you prepared to

37

continue my management. You have now been married three years, and you are safe from the temptations to extravagance which come with the honeymoon. I see that Parisian women, and even titled ones, do manage both their fortunes and their households. Well, as soon as I am certain not so much of your capacity as of your perseverance I shall leave Paris."

"It is Thaddeus of Warsaw, and not that Circus Thaddeus who speaks now," said Clementine. "Go, and come back cured."

"Cured! never," said Paz, his eyes lowered and fixed on Clementine's pretty feet. "You do not know, countess, what charm, what unexpected piquancy of mind she has." Then, feeling his courage fail him, he added hastily, "There is not a woman in society, with her mincing airs, that is worth the honest nature of that young animal."

"At any rate, I wish nothing of the animal about me," said the countess, with a glance like that of an angry viper.

After that evening Comte Paz showed Clementine the exact state of her affairs; he made himself her tutor, taught her the methods and difficulties of the management of property, the proper prices to pay for things, and how to avoid being cheated by her servants. He told her she could rely on Constantin and make him her major-domo. Thaddeus had trained the man thoroughly. By the end of May he thought the countess fully competent to carry on her affairs alone; for Clementine was one of those far-sighted women, full of instinct, who have an innate genius as mistress of a household.

This position of affairs, which Thaddeus had led up to naturally, did not end without further cruel trials; his sufferings were fated not to be as sweet and tender as he was trying to make them. The poor lover forgot to reckon on the hazard of events. Adam fell seriously ill, and Thaddeus, instead of leaving the house, stayed to nurse his friend. His devotion was unwearied. A woman who had any interest in employing her perspicacity might have seen in this devotion a sort of punishment imposed by a noble soul to repress an involuntary evil thought; but women see all, or see nothing, according to the condition of their souls—love is their sole illuminator.

During forty-five days Paz watched and tended Adam without appearing to think of Malaga, for the very good reason that he never did think of her. Clementine, feeling that Adam was at the point of death though he did not die, sent for all the leading doctors of Paris in consultation.

"If he comes safely out of this," said the most distinguished of them all, "it will only be by an effort of nature. It is for those who nurse him to watch for the moment when they must second nature. The count's life is in the hands of his nurses."

Thaddeus went to find Clementine and tell her this result of the consultation. He found her sitting in the Chinese pavilion, as much for a little rest as to leave the field to the doctors and not embarrass them. As he walked along the winding gravelled path which led to the pavilion, Thaddeus seemed to himself in the depths of an abyss described by Dante. The unfortunate man had never dreamed that the possibility might arise of becoming Clementine's husband, and now he had drowned himself in a ditch of mud. His face was convulsed, when he reached the kiosk, with an agony of grief; his head, like Medusa's, conveyed despair.

"Is he dead?" said Clementine.

"They have given him up; that is, they leave him to nature. Do not go in; they are still there, and Bianchon is changing the dressings."

"Poor Adam! I ask myself if I have not sometimes pained him," she said.

"You have made him very happy," said Thaddeus; "you ought to be easy on that score, for you have shown every indulgence for him."

"My loss would be irreparable."

"But, dear, you judged him justly."

"I was never blind to his faults," she said, "but I loved him as a wife should love her husband."

"Then you ought, in case you lose him," said Thaddeus, in a voice which Clementine had never heard him use, "to grieve for him less than if you lost a man who was your pride, your love, and all your life,—as some men are to you women. Surely you can be frank at this moment with a friend like me. I shall grieve, too; long before your marriage I had made him my child, I had sacrificed my life to him. If he dies I shall be without an interest on earth; but life is still beautiful to a widow of twenty-four."

"Ah! but you know that I love no one," she said, with the impatience of grief.

"You don't yet know what it is to love," said Thaddeus.

"Oh, as husbands are, I have sense enough to prefer a child like my poor Adam to a superior man. It is now over a month that we have been saying to each other, 'Will he live?' and these alternations have prepared me, as they have you, for this loss. I can be frank with you. Well, I would give my life to save Adam. What is a woman's independence in Paris? the freedom to let herself be taken in by ruined or dissipated men who pretend to love her. I pray to God to leave me this husband who is so kind, so obliging, so little fault-finding, and who is beginning to stand in awe of me."

"You are honest, and I love you the better for it," said Thaddeus, taking her hand which she yielded to him, and kissing it. "In solemn moments like these there is unspeakable satisfaction in finding a woman without hypocrisy. It is possible to converse with you. Let us look to the future. Suppose that God does not grant your prayer,—and no one cries to him more than I do, 'Leave me my friend!' Yes, these fifty nights have not weakened me; if thirty more days and nights are needed I can give them while you sleep,—yes, I will tear him from death if, as the doctors say, nursing can save him. But suppose that in spite of you and me, the count dies,—well, then, if you were loved, oh, adored, by a man of a heart and soul that are worthy of you—"

"I may have wished for such love, foolishly, but I have never met with it."

"Perhaps you are mistaken—"

Clementine looked fixedly at Thaddeus, imagining that there was less of love than of cupidity in his thoughts; her eyes measured him from head to foot and poured contempt upon him; then she crushed him with the words, "Poor Malaga!" uttered in tones which a great lady alone can find to give expression to her disdain. She rose, leaving Thaddeus half unconscious behind her, slowly re-entered her boudoir, and went back to Adam's chamber.

An hour later Paz returned to the sick-room, and began anew, with death in his heart, his care of the count. From that moment he said nothing. He was forced to struggle with the patient, whom he managed in a way that excited the admiration of the doctors. At all hours his watchful eyes were like lamps always lighted. He showed no resentment to Clementine, and listened to her thanks without accepting them; he seemed both dumb and deaf. To himself he was saying, "She shall owe his life to me," and he wrote the thought as it were in letters of fire on the walls of Adam's room. On the fifteenth day Clementine was forced to give up the nursing, lest she should utterly break down. Paz was unwearied. At last, towards the end of August, Bianchon, the family physician, told Clementine that Adam was out of danger.

"Ah, madame, you are under no obligation to me," he said; "without his friend, Comte Paz, we could not have saved him."

The day after the meeting of Paz and Clementine in the kiosk, the Marquis de Ronquerolles came to see his nephew. He was on the eve of starting for Russia on a secret diplomatic mission. Paz took occasion to say a few words to him. The first day that Adam was able to drive out with his wife and Thaddeus, a gentleman entered the courtyard as the carriage was about to leave it, and asked for Comte Paz. Thaddeus, who was sitting on the front seat of the caleche, turned to take a letter which bore the stamp of the ministry of Foreign affairs. Having read it, he put it into his pocket in a manner which prevented Clementine or Adam from speaking of it. Nevertheless, by the time they reached the porte Maillot, Adam, full of curiosity, used the privilege of a sick man whose caprices are to be gratified, and said to Thaddeus: "There's no indiscretion between brothers who love each other,—tell me what there is in that despatch; I'm in a fever of curiosity."

Clementine glanced at Thaddeus with a vexed air, and remarked to her husband: "He has been so sulky with me for the last two months that I shall never ask him anything again."

"Oh, as for that," replied Paz, "I can't keep it out of the newspapers, so I may as well tell you at once. The Emperor Nicholas has had the grace to appoint me captain in a regiment which is to take part in the expedition to Khiva."

"You are not going?" cried Adam.

"Yes, I shall go, my dear fellow. Captain I came, and captain I return. We shall dine together to-morrow for the last time. If I don't start at once for St. Petersburg I shall have to make the journey by land, and I am not rich, and I must leave Malaga a little independence. I ought to think of the only woman who has been able to understand me; she thinks me grand, superior. I dare say she is faithless, but she would jump—"

"Through the hoop, for your sake and come down safely on the back of her horse," said Clementine sharply.

"Oh, you don't know Malaga," said the captain, bitterly, with a sarcastic look in his eyes which made Clementine thoughtful and uneasy.

"Good-by to the young trees of this beautiful Bois, which you Parisians love, and the exiles who find a home here love too," he said, presently. "My eyes will never again see the evergreens of the avenue de Mademoiselle, nor the acacias nor the cedars of the rond-points. On the borders of Asia, fighting for the Emperor, promoted to the command, perhaps, by force of courage and by risking my life, it may happen that I shall regret these Champs-Elysees where I have driven beside you, and where you pass. Yes, I shall grieve for Malaga's hardness—the Malaga of whom I am now speaking."

This was said in a manner that made Clementine tremble.

"Then you do love Malaga very much?" she asked.

"I have sacrificed for her the honor that no man should ever sacrifice."

"What honor?"

"That which we desire to keep at any cost in the eyes of our idol."

After that reply Thaddeus said no more; he was silent until, as they passed a wooden building on the Champs Elysees, he said, pointing to it, "That is the Circus."

He went to the Russian Embassy before dinner, and thence to the Foreign office, and the next morning he had started for Havre before the count and countess were up.

"I have lost a friend," said Adam, with tears in his eyes, when he heard that Paz had gone,—"a friend in the true meaning of the word. I don't know what has made him abandon me as if a pestilence were in my house. We are not friends to quarrel about a woman," he said, looking intently at Clementine. "You heard what he said yesterday about Malaga. Well, he has never so much as touched the little finger of that girl."

"How do you know that?" said Clementine.

"I had the natural curiosity to go and see Mademoiselle Turquet, and the poor girl can't explain even to herself the absolute reserve which Thad—"

"Enough!" said the countess, retreating into her bedroom. "Can it be that I am the victim of some noble mystification?" she asked herself. The thought had hardly crossed her mind when Constantin brought her the following letter written by Thaddeus during the night:—

"Countess,—To seek death in the Caucasus and carry with me your contempt is more than I can bear. A man should die untainted. When I saw you for the first time I loved you as we love a woman whom we shall love forever, even though she be unfaithful to us. I loved you thus,—I, the friend of the man you had chosen and were about to marry; I, poor; I, the steward,—a voluntary service, but still the steward of your household.

"In this immense misfortune I found a happy life. To be to you an indispensable machine, to know myself useful to your comfort, your luxury, has been the source of deep enjoyments. If these enjoyments were great when I thought only of Adam, think what they were to my soul when the woman I loved was the mainspring of all I did. I have known the pleasures of maternity in my love. I accepted life thus. Like the paupers who live along the great highways, I built myself a hut on the borders of your beautiful domain, though I never sought to approach you. Poor and lonely, struck blind by Adam's good fortune, I was, nevertheless, the giver. Yes, you were surrounded by a love as pure as a guardian-angel's; it waked while you slept; it caressed you with a look as you passed; it was happy in its own existence,—you were the sun of my native land to me, poor exile, who now writes to you with tears in his eyes as he thinks of the happiness of those first days.

"When I was eighteen years old, having no one to love, I took for my ideal mistress a charming woman in Warsaw, to whom I confided all my thoughts, my wishes; I made her the queen of my nights and days. She knew nothing of all this; why should she? I loved my love.

"You can fancy from this incident of my youth how happy I was merely to live in the sphere of your existence, to groom your

horse, to find the new-coined gold for your purse, to prepare the
splendor of your dinners and your balls, to see you eclipsing the
elegance of those whose fortunes were greater than yours, and all
by my own good management. Ah! with what ardor I have ransacked
Paris when Adam would say to me, 'She wants this or that.' It was
a joy such as I can never express to you. You wished for a trifle
at one time which kept me seven hours in a cab scouring the city;
and what delight it was to weary myself for you. Ah! when I saw
you, unseen by you, smiling among your flowers, I could forget
that no one loved me. On certain days, when my happiness turned my
head, I went at night and kissed the spot where, to me, your feet
had left their luminous traces. The air you had breathed was
balmy; in it I breathed in more of life; I inhaled, as they say
persons do in the tropics, a vapor laden with creative principles.

"I *must* tell you these things to explain the strange presumption
of my involuntary thoughts,—I would have died rather than avow it
until now.

"You will remember those few days of curiosity when you wished to
know the man who performed the household miracles you had
sometimes noticed. I thought,—forgive me, madame,—I believed you
might love me. Your good-will, your glances interpreted by me, a
lover, seemed to me so dangerous—for me—that I invented that
story of Malaga, knowing it was the sort of liaison which women
cannot forgive. I did it in a moment when I felt that my love
would be communicated, fatally, to you. Despise me, crush me with
the contempt you have so often cast upon me when I did not deserve
it; and yet I am certain that, if, on that evening when your aunt
took Adam away from you, I had said what I have now written to
you, I should, like the tamed tiger that sets his teeth once more
in living flesh, and scents the blood, and—

                                            "Midnight."

"I could not go on; the memory of that hour is still too living.
Yes, I was maddened. Was there hope for me in your eyes? then
victory with its scarlet banners would have flamed in mine and
fascinated yours. My crime has been to think all this; perhaps
wrongly. You alone can judge of that dreadful scene when I drove
back love, desire, all the most invincible forces of our manhood,
with the cold hand of gratitude,—gratitude which must be eternal.

"Your terrible contempt has been my punishment. You have shown me
there is no return from loathing or disdain. I love you madly. I
should have gone had Adam died; all the more must I go because he
lives. A man does not tear his friend from the arms of death to
betray him. Besides, my going is my punishment for the thought
that came to me that I would let him die, when the doctors said
that his life depended on his nursing.

"Adieu, madame; in leaving Paris I lose all, but you lose nothing
now in my being no longer near you.

"Your devoted

"Thaddeus Paz."

"If my poor Adam says he has lost a friend, what have I lost?" thought
Clementine, sinking into a chair with her eyes fixed on the carpet.

The following letter Constantin had orders to give privately to the count:—

"My dear Adam,—Malaga has told me all. In the name of all your
future happiness, never let a word escape you to Clementine about
your visits to that girl; let her think that Malaga has cost me a
hundred thousand francs. I know Clementine's character; she will

43

never forgive you either your losses at cards or your visits to
Malaga.

"I am not going to Khiva, but to the Caucasus. I have the spleen;
and at the pace at which I mean to go I shall be either Prince
Paz in three years, or dead. Good-by; though I have taken
sixty-thousand francs from Nucingen, our accounts are even.

"Thaddeus."

"Idiot that I was," thought Adam; "I came near to cutting my throat just now, talking about Malaga."

It is now three years since Paz went away. The newspapers have as yet said nothing about any Prince Paz. The Comtesse Laginska is immensely interested in the expeditions of the Emperor Nicholas; she is Russian to the core, and reads with a sort of avidity all the news that comes from that distant land. Once or twice every winter she says to the Russian ambassador, with an air of indifference, "Do you know what has become of our poor Comte Paz?"

Alas! most Parisian women, those beings who think themselves so clever and clear-sighted, pass and repass beside a Paz and never recognize him. Yes, many a Paz is unknown and misconceived, but—horrible to think of!—some are misconceived even though they are loved. The simplest women in society exact a certain amount of conventional sham from the greatest men. A noble love signifies nothing to them if rough and unpolished; it needs the cutting and setting of a jeweller to give it value in their eyes.

In January, 1842, the Comtesse Laginska, with her charm of gentle melancholy, inspired a violent passion in the Comte de La Palferine, one of the most daring and presumptuous lions of the day. La Palferine was well aware that the conquest of a woman so guarded by reserve as the Comtesse Laginska was difficult, but he thought he could inveigle this charming creature into committing herself if he took her unawares, by the assistance of a certain friend of her own, a woman already jealous of her.

Quite incapable, in spite of her intelligence, of suspecting such treachery, the Comtesse Laginska committed the imprudence of going with her so-called friend to a masked ball at the Opera. About three in the morning, led away by the excitement of the scene, Clementine, on whom La Palferine had expended his seductions, consented to accept a supper, and was about to enter the carriage of her faithless friend. At this critical moment her arm was grasped by a powerful hand, and she was taken, in spite of her struggles, to her own carriage, the door of which stood open, though she did not know it was there.

"He has never left Paris!" she exclaimed to herself as she recognized Thaddeus, who disappeared when the carriage drove away.

Did any woman ever have a like romance in her life? Clementine is

44

constantly hoping she may again see Paz.

9 783734 083297